MEATBALL MAN AND HOAGI[E]
THE FUSION OF INCLUSION

WHERE FRIENDS MEAT

WRITTEN BY **MARK GRAHAM, SEAN HANLEY** AND **THE INCLUSION TEAM**

ILLUSTRATED BY **DYANNA ZOLLO**

Meatball Man and Hoagie Boy in The Fusion of Inclusion – Where Friends Meat.

ISBN: 978-1-09830-923-7

Copyright ©2020 by Developmental Fitness Company, LLC.

Illustrations ©2020 by Developmental Fitness Company, LLC.

Requests for information should be addressed to:

Meatball Man and Hoagie Boy

Developmental Fitness Company, LLC, PO Box 1025, North Wales, Pa 19454.

www.meatballmanhoagieboy.com

To Erin… for teaching the world that penguins can actually breakdance.

It was a beautiful day in the town of Mozzarella. This was the home of the famous chef- Meatball Man.
"I am going to bring lunch to my good friend in the city. I will need to stop by the restaurant to pick up some meatballs. They are his favorite. "

Meatball Man strolls down Linguini Lane to his restaurant Café Amice Carne. This is the place where all his friends meet. He is the head chef there.
"I am glad it is not too sunny. I definitely do not want to get too well-done on my way to the city."

Mozzarella's favorite chef arrives at the cafe and he calls for the cook.

"Did you get that order ready yet? I'm going to the city to meet a friend. I am going to bring him lunch. Our meatballs are his favorite."

The cook calls from the back. "Order up! Would you like an extra side of sauce?"

"Absolutely, that would be great. I'm feeling a little extra saucy this morning. As a matter of fact, I've got a fresh coat of marinara on right now," says Meatball Man.

The cook laughs out loud," Hey buddy, you know you are what you eat!"

"Very funny," says Meatball Man. "I would like to stay and talk but I will have to see you tomorrow. I need to roll down to Provolone Station."

Meatball Man takes his order and walks to Provolone Station where he will catch the Parmesan Express.

"I better hurry so I don't miss the train. I hope I make it there in time. I will use my noodle next time and leave earlier."

Meatball Man steps onto the Provolone Platform to buy his train ticket. "It looks really busy today," he says. "I hope I can find a good seat."

Meatball Man stands on the Provolone Platform and he hears the announcements. "This is the 11:38 Parmesan Express to Grand Cheddar Station." The train pulls up and the doors open.

"I feel a little nervous," says Meatball Man to himself as he steps onto the train.

"I have never been to Grand Cheddar Station. I have never been that far from home. "

The Conductor comes on the loudspeaker. "Please take your seat. Next stop Lasagna Lane." Meatball Man takes his seat as the train pulls out of the station.

The train thunders along to many stops. Many passengers get on at Garlic Grove. A parade of people gets on board at Bacon Alley. An entire circus and a baseball team get on at Salami Station. The train is now filled to the brim.

"How will anyone else get on?" thinks Meatball Man as the conductor comes on the speaker.

"Next stop, American Square!"

GARLIC GROVE

BACON ALLEY

SALAMI STATION

Meatball Man looks away from the window to check his ticket. The Parmesan Express slows down and comes to a complete stop at American Square Train Station.

The train doors open. Hoagie Boy is waiting patiently to get on the Parmesan Express. Meatball Man notices that he looks very different. He doesn't look like the people he knows in Mozzarella.

Meatball Man looks at the new passenger with a stare. "He looks so unlike me. He is very odd. I hope he doesn't sit here near me."

Hoagie Boy steps onto the train. He looks around and realizes there are not many places to sit. He also sees Meatball Man looking at him with a funny stare. Hoagie Boy says to himself, "Would you feast your eyes on this? I don't know if I want to sit next to that guy. He keeps staring at me. He looks very strange. Are there any other seats on this train?"

The conductor calls out, "Take your seat. Cheesesteak Avenue is next stop!"

Hoagie Boy sees there is only one seat left. It is next to Meatball Man. Hoagie Boy thinks to himself, "I guess I have to sit next to this guy in order to get to Grand Cheddar Station. There is nowhere else I can sit. He seems a little too saucy. I hope he doesn't get any on me."

Meatball Man turns to look out the window of the train as Hoagie Boy sits next to him.

Meatball Man thinks to himself, "What type of sandwich is this guy? He seems a little too cheesy for me!"

The train begins to pull out of the station.

Hoagie Boy and Meatball Man look at each other. They size each other up for just a moment and then turn away. They do not smile at each other. They do not talk. They still don't look at each other.

Hoagie Boy thinks to himself, "I guess I'm stuck with this guy until Grand Cheddar Station. Have you ever seen sunglasses on a meatball before?"

Meatball Man keeps his sauce to himself. "I bet this guy thinks he is the best thing since sliced bread. I have never seen his kind on the menu."

Meatball Man hears the announcement and gets excited. "Oh, great! My stop is finally here. I cannot wait to get away from this guy. He has mayonnaise in his hair. He is wearing his tomato all wrong."

Hoagie Boy leans half-way off the seat as the train slows down. "I am so glad we are almost at the station. Now I can get away from this guy. He is lost in the sauce."

The Parmesan Express comes to a stop inside Grand Cheddar Station.

Meatball Man quickly remarks, "Excuse me, sir. This is my stop."

"Oh, yes. It is my stop too," says Hoagie Boy.

Neither one of them realized they were getting off at the same stop.

Hoagie Boy scratches his head. "Is he really getting off at the same stop? I hope he is not following me."

Meatball Man rolls his eyes. "How long is this guy going to be around? Can't this sandwich roll in the other direction?"

The doors to the Parmesan Express open and both Meatball Man and Hoagie Boy rush off the train.

And that's how it happened.

CRASH! SPLAT! They run into each other.

Meatball Man's meatballs fly high into the air and land all over Grand Cheddar Station. His friend's special-order meatballs were now mush.

He glanced over at Hoagie Boy who was now half covered in fresh tomato sauce.

Hoagie Boy begins to wipe the sauce from his roll and apologizes. "I am sorry I bumped into you. Those meatballs smell good. Too bad I am wearing them. Now I know what spaghetti feels like."

"You look good with a side of sauce," says Meatball Man as he smiles. "It is good to have a little color. It goes well with your tomato."

Meatball Man suddenly realizes that he needs help. He turns to Hoagie Boy, "I've never been in this station. I am on my way to Pepperoni Park. Do you know where that is? Do you think you can help me?"

"Sure," says Hoagie Boy as he removes the tomato sauce from his roll. "I know where that is. I would be happy to help you get there. Give me just a minute. I need to get used to this new spread. It looks like I am the one lost in the sauce."

Hoagie Boy walks Meatball Man to the far end of Grand Cheddar Station.

Hoagie Boy gives Meatball Man directions. "You want to go up these stairs and walk two blocks. That will take you past Pastrami Place. Make a left and you will see the entrance to Pepperoni Park."

He apologizes to Meatball Man again. "Listen. I am sorry for my clumsiness. It is a shame that you lost your meatballs. I feel like a piece of burnt toast."

Meatball Man laughs. "There is nothing to worry about. Accidents happen. It looks good on you. Now you have red to go with your blue outfit. You definitely make a good role model."

Meatball Man reaches into his pocket and gives Hoagie Boy a card.

"Listen. I have a restaurant in the country. I am the chef. This is my card. Please come for dinner."

Meatball Man continues to smile and laugh. "Dinner is on me next time since my friend's lunch is on you!"

Hoagie Boy thanks Meatball Man. "Wonderful! I haven't been to the country in a long time. I will come to visit. Thank you again."

The two of them shake hands.

They smile at each other and go their separate ways from Grand Cheddar Station.

Meatball Man climbs the exit stairs and walks east towards Pastrami Place.

Hoagie Boy strolls west up Wing Sauce Way from Grand Cheddar Station. He laughs, "I never should have judged him like that. I was wrong about him. What a great guy!"

"I never would have expected him to treat me to dinner after I made him spill his friend's lunch. I will have to roll over to Mozzarella to catch up with him one day."

Meatball Man finds the entrance to Pepperoni Park. He greets his best friend DJ Dog. "What 's up dog?"

DJ Dog gives him a high five. "What's up man? It is good to see you. How are you doing?"

"I'm great but your surprise lunch was knocked out of my hands when I was getting off the train," explains Meatball Man.

DJ Dog shrugs it off. "No worries at all my friend!"

Meatball Man stops and laughs. "I brought you the restaurant meatballs. I know they are your favorite. Right now, they are all over the train station floor. Most of them wound up on this guy that ran into me. Sauce and all. He looks like a four- course meal right now."

DJ Dog chuckles, "That's funny. Hey, come with me. I want you to meet a friend of mine."

Hoagie Boy finally arrives at Kid Burger's Music Studio at the corner of Swiss Road and Fifth Avenue. Kid Burger notices Hoagie Boy's new color. "What happened to you? I didn't know you came with a side of sauce. What kind of sandwich are you today?"

"I was in a rush to get here and I ran into a guy coming off the train. He was carrying meatballs and sauce. We crashed into each other and they went all over the train station floor. I got covered in the sauce", explained Hoagie Boy.

Kid Burger laughed. "You look very patriotic with an extra side of sauce. You were just white and blue. Now you are red, white and blue just like my guitar!"

"Very funny, friend" said Hoagie Boy.

Kid Burger finishes laughing. "Listen. Come walk with me. I want you to meet a friend of mine. You can bring your side of sauce along too."

Meanwhile, Meatball Man and DJ Dog arrive at the Sausage Stage inside Pepperoni Park.

DJ Dog explains to his friend, "I need some help setting up for a show today. Would you like to help me out on stage?"

"Of course," replied Meatball Man. "That sounds great. What type of show is going on today?"

DJ Dog smiled and explained. "Today we are going to play the songs that make us belong."

Kid Burger and Hoagie Boy also find themselves walking towards Sausage Stage inside Pepperoni Park.
Kid Burger yells to his good friend. "Hey Mr. DJ. What's up Dog? It is good to see you my friend!"

"Hello music man, "says DJ Dog. "It is good to see you. I see you brought a friend."
Kid Burger replies, "Yes, this is my friend from American Square."
"Fantastic!" says DJ Dog. "Now it is a party. Let's get started."

Meatball Man and Hoagie Boy see each other from across Sausage Stage.
They look at each other and smile. They both start laughing. They had met only moments
ago. Now they know they have the same friends.

Hoagie Boy leans over to DJ Dog. "Hey, that's the guy I ran into coming off the train."
"Yes sir. It is!", says Meatball Man as he walks over. "You still look good with a side of
sauce!"

Hoagie Boy jokes. "That is food for thought. I am glad that I have a role here."

"I think it is pretty cool we have the same friends ", Meatball Man says to Hoagie Boy.
"Don't you?"

DJ Dog starts to spin records while Kid Burger gets on the microphone.

Meatball Man stands next to Hoagie Boy and puts his arm around him. "It just goes to show you that we are all friends in the end."
Kid Burger strums his newly tuned guitar. "It's fusion by inclusion baby!" he says.

Hoagie Boy agrees and smiles. "Definitely. It's how we roll!"
"It's where friends meat!" says Meatball Man.

DJ Dog gets the music started. "Alright my friends. Now we are the food with the mood. Everybody dance now."
All the friends smiled. All the friends laughed. All the friends danced.
And they all did it together.

THE INCLUSION TEAM

I am Mark. I am Meatball Man. My best friend is DJ Dog. I have two jobs. I work at a supermarket helping customers. I also work with a caterer. I help with food preparation and delivery set up. I participate in Special Olympics. I compete in bocce, floor hockey, soccer and basketball. I am also a powerlifter. I enjoy Philadelphia Phillies and Philadelphia Eagles games and dances with my friends' and girlfriend Kelly. I like to spend time at friends' houses. I enjoy cooking meatloaf or stir fry dinners for my family.

IT'S WHERE FRIENDS MEAT

Meatball Man

I am Sean. I am Hoagie Boy. Kid Burger is my son. I am the founder of Developmental Fitness Company. I work as a Physical Therapist (DPT) and as a Licensed Athletic Trainer (ATC). I coach Special Olympics basketball and powerlifting. I competed as a powerlifter and a runner. I enjoy Villanova University basketball, coaching, the Muppets, 80's music and helping others.

THAT'S HOW WE ROLL

Hoagie Boy

Join
THE INCLUSION TEAM
AT
WWW.MEATBALLMANHOAGIEBOY.COM
FACEBOOK @MEATBALLMANHOAGIEBOY

I am Joe. I am DJ Dog. My best friend is Meatball Man. He has been my best friend since elementary school. We like to hang out, play video games and compete in Special Olympics. We are bocce champions! We like to go to Philadelphia Eagles, Philadelphia Phillies and Philadelphia Flyers games. We laugh a lot. Our favorite thing is our week at Special Olympics sports camp. We love to dance. Everybody dance now!

EVERYBODY DANCE NOW!

DJ Dog

I am Kieran. I am Kid Burger. Hoagie Boy is my dad. I am eight years old. I am the official musician of The Inclusion Team. I am a second grader and a guitar player. I compete in basketball, lacrosse and swimming. I really enjoy music. My favorite subject is math. I also participate in Cub Scouts. I would like to be an astronaut one day. I like being Kid Burger because music can connect everyone.

IT'S FUSION BY INCLUSION BABY!

Kid Burger

I am Dyanna. I am the illustrator. I am an artist and graphic designer by night and work as a director by day. I went to school for Interactive Media and I spend my summers painting murals. I live in a house in the country with my husband and my cat. I enjoy playing video games and spending time with my friends and family.

47